The New Blue Tractor

Written by Stacey Gabel
Illustrated by Richard Neuman

To my son and his love of tractors. - S.G.
To my grandfather who taught me to drive a tractor. - R.N.

First published by Dog Ear Publishing
4010 W. 86th Street, Ste H
Indianapolis, IN 46268
www.dogearpublishing.net

ISBN: 978-159858-424-0
Library of Congress Control Number: 2007938382

This book is printed on acid-free paper.
This book is a work of Fiction. Places, events, and situations in this book are purely Fictional and any resemblance to actual persons, living or dead, is coincidental.

Printed in the United States of America

The blue tractor stood shiny and new.

3

A man paid for the tractor.

He took it to a farm to work.

The tractor gets hooked to the plow.

The tractor helps plow the field.

The tractor gets
hooked to the
corn planter.

8

The blue tractor helps plant the corn field. 9

The tractor is dirty.
The tractor gets a wash.

The tractor looks shiny and new again.

12   The corn is ready to be picked.

The tractor pulls the wagon.

The corn fills the wagon.

The tractor takes the red wagon
filled with corn to the grain bin.

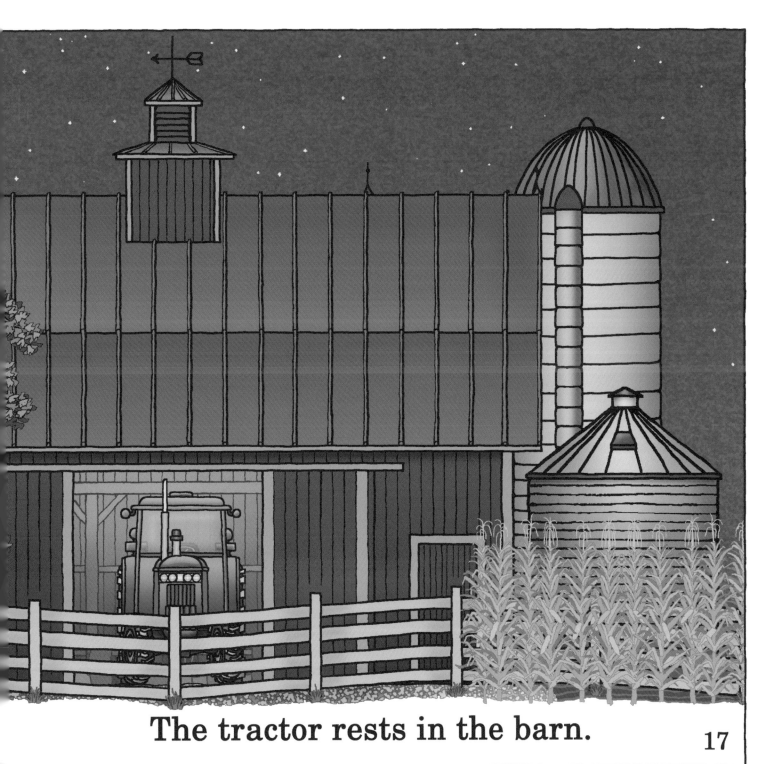

The tractor rests in the barn.

17

The tractor helps at the farm.

The tractor pushes snow in the winter.

20 The tractor has a tire that needs fixed.

It is getting warm in the spring.

Soon the blue tractor
will work in the field again.

Nuts and Bolts

Name some of the items in the story
that you find on a farm.

Do you see any tractors
working in the fields where you live?
What is the tractor doing in the field?

How many syllables are in the words
"tractor", "plow", "wagon", and "silo"?
Clap your hands to help you count them.

What kind of work will the tractor do
after the story ends?

Retell the story of "The New Blue Tractor"
to a person in your family.

CPSIA information can be obtained at www.ICGtesting.com
Printed in the USA
BVIW12n0516101217
502400BV00009B/491